The Old Ones Told Me

American Indian Stories
for Children

As told and illustrated by

Berry Keeper

Binford & Mort Publishing

Portland, Oregon

THE OLD ONES TOLD ME

American Indian Stories for Children

Copyright © 1989 by Binford & Mort Publishing

Printed in the United States of America

ISBN: 0-8323-0473-5

First Edition 1989
Second Printing 1992

In Memory of
my Cherokee Grandparents
Richard and Frances Berry
and my friend Fanny Cope

Acknowledgements

My many thanks to my daughters Jennifer and Jessica,
for constantly asking to hear the old stories of their heritage,
to my husband Rand, to my dad Sam, for helping me learn
to use that silly computer, to Bob Manseth of Indian Forest, who
loaned me his massive research library on the American Indian
and served as my historical consultant, and to my mom Ruby,
without whom this book wouldn't be possible.

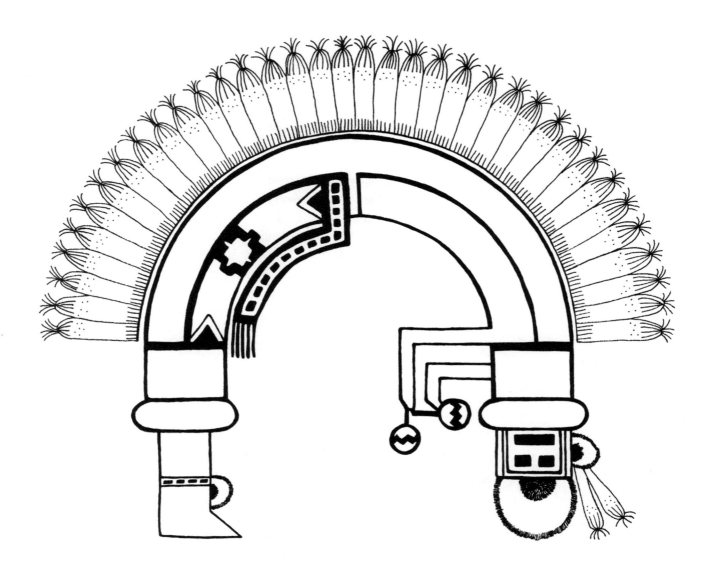

A Corn Dancer

Bowing in ceremony, he prays for corn to grow. Stalks of corn are on his back. The rabbit fur on his moccasins and headdress are for luck. The breechcloth protects his groins so that he will be fertile. The rattles show that it is a ceremony.

Contents

The Storyteller
The old man tells his family stories that he was told as a child. Most American Indian stories
start with "The old ones told me . . ." or "I was told by my elders when I was a child . . . ."

Foreword

The stories told around the fire in the evenings, hundreds of years ago, are among the masterpieces of the American Indian, and every bit as much art and culture as their counterparts, the fairy tales.

True enough, modern civilzation has forgotten many of the old stories, and created new ones, but also as true, is the fact that many people know an Indian story or two from their childhood, but fail to recognize it.

One of my favorite examples of this, is the classic poem, "Rock-A-Bye-Baby."

> Rock-a-bye baby
> in the tree top
> when the wind blows
> the cradle will rock.
> When the bough breaks
> the cradle will fall
> and down will come baby
> cradle and all.

Many people have wondered what the cradle was doing in the tree to start with! Modern artists have depicted as old fashioned English-Dutch rocking cradle in the top of a tall tree.

Doesn't make much sense, does it?

No. Not until you realize that the cradle, is a cradle-board, used by American Indian women to carry their infants on their back while traveling. When they stopped to rest, the cradle-board and the sleeping baby were hung on a low branch facing away from the wind. The wind pushing on the back of the cradle-board rocked the infant in a way that felt much like the mother was still walking.

I hope that you will enjoy these other stories from America's original citizens!

Where the Dog Ran

Cherokee

A long time ago in a small village, the Cherokee people woke up from their night's sleep, to find that all of their breakfast was gone. They were very confused.

While the adults talked, the children got their picking baskets, and started to leave the meal house to pick berries, when one little boy noticed giant dog tracks!

The dog tracks were almost as large as the meal house itself!

After much discussion, it was decided that all of the people would bring a noisemaker, and frighten the giant dog, so that it would not want to return.

That night, all of the people hid in the darkness to wait for the giant dog.

When the sky was the darkest, a giant dog appeared from the west, and began to eat their meal.

The chief was so frightened that he almost forgot to give the signal to attack! But upon the lowering of his hand, the people of the village began to beat their drums and shake their rattles.

This startled the giant dog, who turned and jumped high into the sky, dropping bits of the food from his mouth, creating a great white trail called "Gil' LiUtsun' Stanun'yi," which means "Where The Dog Ran."

The white man calls this the "Milky Way."

A Raven Dancer
This man's dance tells the story of Raven, a trickster who stole the sun. The man wears a Raven raiment with the sun represented by a ball in the beak.

Raven Steals The Sun

Intertribal

It is told that at the beginning of the Earth, there was a very powerful chief, who lived in the sky.

This chief was very greedy and liked to keep everything for himself. One of the finest possessions he held was the sun, which he kept in a beautiful box, ornamented with wonderful stones and precious metals.

Because the chief kept the sun hidden, the world was always dark.

One night, Raven was flying past the chief's house, and saw the beautiful box by the fire.

Raven sat on the smoke hole and thought about how he might have a few of the shiny stones for his nest, for he loved shiny things very much.

Raven then saw that the house was empty, so he hopped in, and began to peck at the stones. Raven pecked so hard, that the box sprang open!

The sun looked like a wonderful piece for his nest, so Raven quickly picked it up in his beak, and flew out into the sky.

The chief saw Raven as he was going overhead and shouted at Raven so loudly that Raven dropped the sun right there in the middle of the sky!

The Indians will tell you that this story is true. The proof is, that the sun is still in the sky, right where Raven dropped it!

The Princess and the Mouse Woman
The beautiful Princess Rhpisunt took her woolen hair decoration and gave it to the Mouse Woman. The name Mouse Woman is given to women who are known to be particularly clever.

The Story of Mother Bear

Haida

Many years ago, a Haida princess named Rhpisunt was walking in the forest of a nearby island with two of her helpers.

The women had gone far into the woods when they came upon a nicely trimmed path, plentiful with berries. Thinking that this must be a magical path, the girls were not surprised to find that on the ground a bear's pawprints had turned into a man's footprints.

Rhpisunt began to laugh at the bears, calling them silly animals, and quite stupid, since they were not smart enough to know if they were human beings or bears!

Her helpers warned her not to curse the bear, especially on a magical trail in the woods, but the princess was very haughty and would not be silent, and grew much louder.

Having filled the berry baskets, Rhpisunt and her helpers started back to their canoe when the princess, who was following behind her helpers, disappeared.

Rhpisunt found herself in the underground home of the Bear people and was escorted to the tribal council house. Many bears had heard the princess call them stupid, and they were angry.

A mouse woman came to the princess and whispered to her that she would help the princess if the princess would give her a piece of wool for a nest.

From her hair, Rhpisunt took a beautiful hair decoration made of wool and gave it to the small mouse woman.

The little mouse woman was very clever and went to sit between the chief and his son.

"How beautiful the princess is," observed the little mouse woman. "Nowhere in the world have I ever laid eyes on one so lovely. Surely your highness would be admired by all of the forest if you could change her heart to be kind."

The Bear chief thought about this and asked his son's opinion on the matter.

The chief's son saw that Rhpisunt was sorry and he fell in love with her at once, and they were married.

The following spring, Rhpisunt told her husband that she was going to have his children and that she wished to be near her own mother.

Rhpisunt's husband loved her very much, and saw that she was not happy in the land of the Bear people, so he asked the mouse woman to make a magical grease to rub on her skin, which would allow Rhpisunt to leave the land of the Bear people.

The mouse woman did this, because Rhpisunt had been very kind to her, and soon the couple was free from the land of the Bear people.

Rhpisunt returned to Haida with her husband, and in the spring, gave birth to twin cubs.

Rhpisunt was again a Haida princess, and her sons, who like their father's family, could take their bear coverings off and become human-like when in need, became great and admired hunters of the Haida people, and brought great fortune to their tribe.

It is because of this relationship to the bears, that the Haida people call themselves the Bear Clan.

A Northwest Coast Raven

The small slit on top of his head represents an ear. The eye is on the left topside of the head. The beak is pointed and located to the right of the eye. The body and wing are combined and are located in the middle section. The bottom part of the Raven is feathers. Raven is neither good nor bad in American Indian mythology. He is a trickster, and very self-centered. There are probably more legends of Raven than of any other creature.

Raven And The Fisherman

Intertribal

One day, Raven flew into a small fishing village. The fishermen had just returned with their catch for the day. In the bottom of one of the canoes, Raven spied a large basket full of flounder, which was one of his favorite foods. Now it was almost impossible for Raven to get a flounder out of the sea, but Raven set his mind, right then and there, that he would have a dinner of fine flounder!

Raven knew the men in the canoes would never surrender such a fine catch to him willingly, but Raven had a plan.

Raven flew quickly to a meadow, where he knew a family of robins lived, and stole a beak full of the brightest red feathers and stuck them in his head. He then flew down the smoke hole of the fishermen's lodge to show the bright feathers to the wives. The wives all wanted a red feather for their own hair, and asked Raven to bring them some. Raven said that he could not possibly carry that many feathers, but he would gladly show them where they could get their own feathers, if they would follow him.

The wives asked their husbands to take them in their canoes to look for the beautiful red feathers. But the husbands, fearing that it was one of Raven's tricks, told the wives, that they alone would go to look for the feathers, while the wives stayed behind to guard the fish.

The fishermen followed Raven, deeper and deeper into the forest streams, until they were quite lost, then Raven slipped away, and flew quickly back to the village.

Raven then changed himself into the image of the fisherman who had caught the flounder. A fisherman's wife was quite sure that it was her husband who had returned home, so she thought it only natural that he would go straight to the special pool where the best fish were preserved and take out some of them to cook for himself. As Raven finished eating all of the flounder, the village men returned, angry that they had been fooled.

The men chased Raven until they caught him, and shook him until he couldn't move, then they threw him into the water.

The drifting body was then swallowed by an enormous halibut, but Raven resumed his own shape, and so tormented the fish from inside his belly, that the fish swam ashore, and was caught up by the villagers. When the people cut open the fish, Raven burst out, cawed loudly, and flew away with the large fish in his smiling beak.

The Mermaid

Coos

Many years ago, in a village on the ocean, a young woman lived in a fine house with her five brothers.

The brothers thought that it was long past the time that their sister should choose a husband, but the sister said that she would not marry until she had fallen in love.

The woman liked to spend time alone, especially near the ocean.

One evening as she was returning home, a handsome young man appeared beside her and asked if he could walk with her.

"I live in a village at the bottom of the sea," the young man told her. "I have been watching you for several weeks. Will you marry me, and live with me in my village?"

"Oh no," said the young woman, "I could never live so far away from my brothers."

"I would let you visit your brothers as often as you like," promised the young man.

"I will consider your proposal," the young woman answered. "Meet me here by the ocean every day for one year, and that will prove to me that you love me."

"And how will I know that you love me?" questioned the young man.

"I will only marry the man that I love," the young woman said. "If I marry you at the end of the year, you will know that I love you."

The man agreed to this, and at the end of the year, the two were married.

The wedding took place in the man's village, and as a wedding gift, the villagers gave the woman a beautiful undersea tail which resembled a lobster's tail.

The couple lived happily ever after in the ocean village, and the woman visited her brothers many times.

Raven Helps

Siuslaw

One morning, very early, a band of fishermen went up the river to look for a new fishing spot. They had taken several side streams, and had become lost.

Raven was flying overhead and saw that the canoe had come to the end of a small stream, and had become entangled in the weeds.

Raven thought that this was funny, and he flew down and perched himself on the bow of the canoe.

The men were angry because they looked so foolish, and because they thought that Raven was laughing at them. They shooed Raven off of the canoe, and said, "Stay off of our canoe you dumb bird. We have enough trouble now! Can't you see that we're lost? Go away!"

Raven's feelings were hurt, and he spread his wings to fly back into the morning sky. But the chief stopped him, by saying, "Wait Raven, don't let them talk to you like that! Show them that you are as wise as you are beautiful! Prove to them that you are smarter than they are. They are lost and cannot find their way home. Show them that you can! Then they will know that your are indeed smarter than they are!"

Now Raven, who was quite vain, thought about this, and said that he would prove that he was the smarter one, and flew up into the colored sky until he could easily see the streams. He then guided the men in the canoe safely home.

The fishermen never again called the bird dumb, for they now realized that each creature has it's own special powers, and is a worthwhile being.

The Opossum's Tail

Cherokee

Many years ago, Opossum had a long, bushy tail, and he was very proud of it.

Opossum used to make up songs about his beautiful bushy tail, and dance around the fire in the evening, and boast about his tail.

Now Rabbit, who had no tail since the Bear had pulled it out, became very jealous of Opossum, and set out to play a trick on him.

There was to be a great Pow-Wow in the forest, and all of the forest animals were given duties. Rabbit's duty was to tell all of the animals about it.

Rabbit was passing by Opossum's home, so he stopped in to ask him if he was going to come and dance at the Pow-Wow.

Opossum said that he would come only if he could have a special seat, because, as he explained, "I have the most beautiful tail in the world, and it is your duty to sit me where everyone can see me."

Rabbit promised to attend to it for him, and also to send someone to comb and bead the Opossum's tail, so that he would be at his best.

This pleased Opossum, and he agreed to come.

The next stop for Rabbit was to be Cricket's house. Cricket was such an expert hair cutter that the forest animals all called him the barber, but Cricket was also a trickster and did not like Opossum's constant bragging.

The next morning, Cricket went to Opossum's house and began to comb and wrap Opossum's tail. It took a long time, and all the while, all Opossum could talk about was his tail, and how much better it was than any other tail in the forest. Cricket told Opossum that he would wrap his tail with red string, so that it would stay nice until that evening, which was the Pow-Wow, but in truth, Cricket was cutting the hair off of Opossum's tail, very close to the roots!

At the Pow-Wow, Opossum loosened the string from his tail, and stepped into the middle of the floor and began to dance and sing about his beautiful tail. In fact, Opossum became so conceited about his tail, that he wouldn't let any of the other animals sing or dance at all.

Soon Opossum noticed that all of the other animals were laughing! He looked back at them, and wondered what they were laughing at.

Then he looked down at his beautiful tail, and saw that there was not a hair left on it anywhere! It looked more like the tail of a lizard than of an Opossum!

Opossum was so ashamed that he didn't say a word, but rolled over on his back and grinned, as Opossums do when they are taken by surprise.

Now Rabbit and Cricket offered to put the hair back on Opossum's tail for him, but Opossum said no. Opossum had discovered that with his tail hairless, people would smile at him, and laugh with him, and make jokes with him, and since he couldn't brag any longer about his bushy tail, maybe he would also make friends.

So to this day, Opossum has kept his bare tail, his funny grin, and his sense of humor.

The Moose Steps on the Catfish
This style of art is called pictographic and is sometimes found on rocks or the walls of caves.

The Catfish

Menomini

Once, when the Earth was new, Catfish were attractive fish, with rounded heads and smooth faces, much like any other fish. One day, when they were gathered in the water, their chief said to them, "I am tired of being like all of the other fish in the water; let us try and be like the humans, and kill a forest animal for our supper, then all of the other fish in the water will fear us, and know that we are superior." The Catfish listened to this, and prepared hunting spears for themselves while the chief continued to speak. The chief said, "I have often seen a moose come to the edge of the water to eat grass there; let us watch for him, he always comes to the grass when the sun has started into the sky for a little while. We will hide in the rushes, and when he bends down to eat, we will spear him."

When the time came, and the moose bent down near the water, the Catfish all threw spears into his leg. This didn't hurt the moose very much, but it did make him quite angry.

Looking down, the moose saw the Catfish, and began to trample them with his hoofs. The Catfish swam down the river as fast as they could, and to this day they still carry spears with them, and their heads have never quite recovered from the flattening they received when they were trampled into the mud by the moose.

A Northwest Coast Thunderbird
The Thunderbird is holding the Sea Monster in his talons. The face on the Sea Monster is the
face of the artist.

Thunderbird

Quillayute

There was at one time, a terrible storm that lasted for a long time. The storm was caused by an unusually large and evil Sea Monster, who looked very much like a Killer Whale.

The sky was loud with the storm. Rain, hail and sleet came down to the land and ruined the crops. Snow and ice came next, and froze the water so that no one could fish. Even the sea itself was frozen still. Times were hard, and the people were afraid, and went into the council house to speak to the Great Spirit, who had been kind to them since the beginning of life.

When the people had finished, they sat in silence for many hours. No one spoke.

Soon there came a great noise. The unmistakeable sound of great beating of wings was heard in the sky!

The people ran out into the darkness, and from the home of the setting sun, they saw a giant Thunderbird coming toward them with the evil Sea Monster in its talons!

This bird was larger than anyone had ever imagined before! It was an unnatural creature, but kind. It had a large curving beak, a curling appendage on his head, and eyes that glowed like the fire in the sunrise!

Thunderbird softly dropped the evil Sea Monster in the very center of the village, and flew back into the thunder from where it came!

The people knew that the Great Spirit had heard their voices, and were filled with joy. Never again would the evil Sea Monster torment the land, for he was eaten that night, in a wonderful feast of the people.

Collecting Sap from Maple Trees
Sap is gathered from the trees by means of a trough and a basket. It is then boiled and made into maple syrup.

The Arrival Of Maple Sugar

Chippewa

One afternoon, a magical boy named Wenebojo was standing under a maple tree, when suddenly it began to sprinkle maple syrup from it's branches!

Wenebojo knew the value of work, and that if his people were given the maple syrup too easily, they would not appreciate it as much, so he threw away the syrup.

The syrup landed in the top of one of the tallest maple trees, and scattered magical rain over all the trees, dissolving the sugar as it flowed into the tree bark.

Wenebojo's grandmother had been watching her grandson play with the trees. She showed him a way to insert a small piece of wood into each maple tree so that the sap could run down into the vessels beneath.

After much thought, and many days, Wenebojo told the Chippewa tribe that he had decided that they could work for the sweet syrup from the maple trees in this manner.

Now the Chippewa take great pride in the skill of cutting wood, making vessels, and collecting the sap from the trees, to boil it for a long time. This teaches the people that if they work hard, good things will come.

The Love of Feather Cloud

Paiute

Many generations ago, in the days of my great-grandfather, the Paiutes held all of the land from the Columbia River to below the Humboldt; all of Nevada, California and Southern Oregon. The forests gave plenty of food and furs and the people were happy. This was the way until their enemy, the Snakes, conquered them and pushed then back into the desert of the Humboldt.

The chief of the Paiute Nation had a beautiful daughter named Feather Cloud. She was given her name because of a small white cloud which was seen at her birth. She was very neat and clean and her hair was shiny black as a raven's back. She had large bright eyes and a kind and laughing spirit, but would always look down with bashfulness when in camp or among the men or elders. She could sew with the deer sinew and tan buckskin, and always kept her father's moccasins clean and soft. She could make the finest baskets out of the hazel and willow twigs, or of the rye grass and the maidenhair fern stems. Her father was wealthy, but he was constantly offered more wealth for the hand of his beautiful daughter in marriage, which he always refused, saying that she will marry whom she chooses.

In the tribe, but living in another band, was a young man named Red Bear. He was tall, handsome, and braver than an eagle. He looked a person in the eye when he spoke. He was not afraid of anyone. He had no family, but he had been taught the ways of the Paiute by his tribe. He would spend his days hunting in the forests. When he killed more than he needed, he would give the hides and meat to the old people of the tribe, and sometimes ask an old woman to make him some new leggings or a coat. Everyone liked Red Bear, but he was different, and so they were afraid of him.

One afternoon, Red Bear was bringing back a bear from a hunting trip, when he heard singing coming from the clearing. He stood as still as the wolf, and watched Feather Cloud as she made wreaths of flowers. The young maidens were having the Wreath Feast to celebrate her coming into womanhood. Red Bear watched her as she laughed and danced. She was the most beautiful woman in the world to Red Bear, and he left his heart with her from that day on. Red Bear did not speak to her, for men are not allowed at the wreath games, but when the games had ended, he approached her and laid the bearskin at her feet.

That night the great fires were lit, and the whole tribe came to watch Feather Cloud dance and celebrate the end of the feast. Red Bear watched her every move, only the family was allowed to take part in the celebration. Feather Cloud saw Red Bear, and knew that he was to be her future husband. That night, as was the custom, Red Bear went to the no-o-pee of Feather Cloud's father, and sat like a statue at her feet. He did not speak to her yet, because at such a time, no one must speak in the no-o-pee. It would have been wrong by tradition to offer him any hospitality or to even acknowledge him, because he was now a suitor.

The next day, the chief found Red Bear and told him that he disapproved of this courtship. The chief of the Paiutes explained to Red Bear, "The wolf seeks a mate in his own band, and the beaver seeks a mate in his own village. You are not born of my village. Wounded Elk is to be my son. He has many relatives who will give him horses, and will make him a skin no-o-pee. They will fight our enemy for him. He will need these things to become chief." "Wounded Elk is lazy," said Red Bear. "Do you not know that I am the best provider in my village? I will give Feather Cloud a skin no-o-pee, and she will have horses of her own, and she will have skins of the otter and sable to wear!"

That afternoon, Feather Cloud and Red Bear walked along the waters edge for many hours without speaking. Red Bear looked into her eyes and spoke first, "Your father is not pleased that I have no wealth. Does he think that you would ever go hungry? Does he think that your life with me would be poor? You are all that I see in my eyes. You shall be my wife and I shall provide you with anything that your heart desires. You shall bear to me many children, and they will live in a no-o-pee filled with love. These things that your father wants are easy to get. I will go into the woods and return again for you, bringing all that your father wants and more. Will you wait for me?" "My dear Red Bear," spoke Feather Cloud as she raised her eyes to his, "you are dearer to me than my own hand. I will wait for you."

Many days passed and no word was heard from Red Bear, and the heart of Feather Cloud was heavy. Her father spoke to her saying, "Red Bear has gone, and will not return. You must think of marriage now. See how patient Wounded Elk is?" Feather Cloud looked again at the ground and said to her father, "Tell me what I have done that you will not let me stay in your no-o-pee with you." The chief's heart was softened and he kissed her cheek. "You shall marry whom you choose my child," said the chief.

Many more days passed, and Wounded Elk's family brought many horses and furs to the chief, saying that they wished the marriage of Wounded Elk and Feather Cloud to take place. The old chief spoke to his daughter saying, "Now I will give you to Wounded Elk whether it pleases you or not." Feather Cloud fell into the dust and cried, "What is it that I have done that you like horses and furs better than me?" Her father replied, "Very well my daughter, you need not go with him if you are so strongly against it, but listen, I tell you now that you may attend the Feast of the Autumns with the maidens, but if by the Midwinter Festival, Red Bear has not returned for you, you will be wed to Wounded Elk."

The time of the Feast of the Autumns had come and the people gathered nuts and seeds, roots and wild anise roots with camas and many others. They ate no meat of any kind, because they had meat all year around, and it did not belong to Autumn. Feather Cloud was bringing one of her beautiful baskets full of roasted nuts to the meal table when in front of her eyes, an arrow flew into her father's side! The Snakes had attacked from the north! It was a quick attack, and soon the enemy had retreated. Feather Cloud had taken the arrow out of her father and stopped the hole with fresh pitch from a pine tree, and owl feathers from her basket. There was a young Snake taken captive, who told the Paiute chief that Wounded Elk had paid them to attack the camp on this morning, and to kill the chief so that he could marry the chief's daughter and become chief himself. Before the young Snake was able to give his proof, Wounded Elk ran up behind the man and knocked him unconscious with a war club. The man later disappeared in the night.

The day had come for the Midwinter Festival, and still no one had heard from Red Bear. The chief told Feather Cloud that she must choose a husband in the morning. If she did not choose, he would give her to Wounded Elk. Feather Cloud was so upset that she ran into the woods and hid, but she was found the next day and brought to her father.

In the evening the fires were built high, and the pipes were made to send out blue smoke. The flutes were playing love songs and the drummers were drumming. Each suitor for Feather

Cloud would dance in the middle of the circle and tell of the things that he had done. Wounded Elk told of how he had killed an elk with only a knife, and how he had hit the captive. These were the finest things that he had done. When he had finished, a young man stepped into the circle with a great war bonnet on that covered his face, and began to dance. He was beautiful and dark like the black wolf. When he danced, the muscles moved as if he was a cougar. As he spoke, the heart of Feather Cloud jumped. "I am Paiute!" he said, "and I have the heart of a man! I do not talk of killing elk, that is to get food. A boy can get food. I have gone across the mountains to where the land meets the sky, and there is the end of the world! I found a party of Crows on the warpath. They were coming here. I fought them while we were riding and turned the living ones away! I took their horses and hid in the rocks. I then found buffalo in a large valley, and I rode to the head of the herd and killed the finest ones, until I had more meat and robes than I wanted. Then I hid my horses and went among the Blackfeet and traded for some fine blankets made from goat's hair. Then I loaded my herd of horses with jerked buffalo and robes and blankets and some fine bows and goods, and came among the Snakes. They did not know me to be a Paiute. There I heard Wounded Elk talk of killing the chief of the Paiutes! I have returned for my bride!" Then the young man who had been dancing, stopped in front of Wounded Elk, and threw off his war bonnet! It was Red Bear! Wounded Elk ran so far that not even the Blackfeet ever saw him again.

Red Bear went to where Feather Cloud sat with her head to the ground. He turned to her father and spoke. "I have more horses and wealth than anyone, and from your relatives I ask nothing." The chief replied, "I will give you my war-bow, and you shall be my son." A bowl was put in the hands of Feather Cloud, filled with roasted acorns. She offered the bowl to Red Bear, but he took her by the wrist and drew her to him. Then he fed her some of the acorns and ate some himself, and so they were married.

Red Bear became the greatest chief of the Paiutes, and drove back their enemies until they had regained all of the land that they had lost. Feather Cloud and Red Bear were happy, and the old people gave their advice on how they should live.

Front Cover:
A Northwest Coast Sea Monster
It is called a Sisutl, and guards the homes of the Underwater Dwellers like whales and mermaids.

Back Cover:
The Eagle
The traditional American Indian believes that his prayers ride on the wings of eagles and are delivered in this way to God; therefore, the eagle is a sacred animal.